For Tom and Jane
—J.B.

For Ed Koren
—H.B.

THIS IS A BORZOI BOOK PUBLISHED BY ALFRED A. KNOPF

Text copyright © 2016 by Jeanne Birdsall

Jacket art and interior illustrations copyright © 2016 by Harry Bliss

All rights reserved. Published in the United States by Alfred A. Knopf, an imprint of Random House Children's Books,
a division of Penguin Random House LLC, New York.

Knopf, Borzoi Books, and the colophon are registered trademarks of Penguin Random House LLC.

Visit us on the Web! randomhousekids.com

Educators and librarians, for a variety of teaching tools, visit us at RHTeachersLibrarians.com

Library of Congress Cataloging-in-Publication Data

Birdsall, Jeanne.

My favorite pets by Gus W. for Ms. Smolinski's class / by Jeanne Birdsall ; illustrated by Harry Bliss. — First edition.

p. cm.

Summary: In his homework assignment, Gus spends less time on what he likes about sheep and more on how he has
gotten in trouble doing such things as using a sheep as an umbrella, or letting sheep into his house.

ISBN 978-0-385-75570-2 (trade) — ISBN 978-0-385-75571-9 (lib. bdg.) — ISBN 978-0-385-75572-6 (ebook)

[1. Sheep—Fiction. 2. Behavior—Fiction. 3. Humorous stories.] I. Bliss, Harry, illustrator. II. Title.

PZ7.B51197My 2016   [E]—dc23   2014033875

The illustrations in this book were created using black India ink and watercolor.

MANUFACTURED IN CHINA

July 2016   10 9 8 7 6 5 4 3 2 1   First Edition

Random House Children's Books supports the First Amendment and celebrates the right to read.

MY FAVORITE PETS

BY GUS W.
FOR MS. SMOLINSKI'S CLASS

WORDS BY **JEANNE BIRDSALL**

PICTURES BY **HARRY BLISS**

ALFRED A. KNOPF · NEW YORK

My favorite pet is sheep. We have seventeen in our yard. Seventeen sheep are still sheep, not sheeps.

A boy sheep is a ram. He has horns.

The horns do not come off.

A girl sheep is a ewe. If you say,
"Hey, Ewe," she won't answer.
Even if you shout it.

A baby sheep is a lamb. If you trade your little brother for a lamb, your mother will say,

Sheep look silly with pajamas on their heads, especially your little brother's favorite porpoise pajamas.

They also look silly in a scarf and will wreck it. Your mother will say,

GUS, ISN'T THAT THE SCARF MS. SMOLINSKI LOANED YOU WHEN YOU LOST YOURS?

CHOMP CHOMP

Sheep live outside, even when it rains. If you use a sheep for an umbrella, your father will say,

Sheep have wool instead of hair.
If you cut some off, your mother
will say,

You're too big to ride on sheep, but your little brother isn't. He will cry, and your father will say,

Sheep won't ride a skateboard, no matter how long you teach them.

Or a bicycle.

They also will not climb a tree.

You can't put sheep
into a wheelbarrow.

You can't put them into a car.
Even a big car.

You can get sheep into your house.

But they won't like the kitchen.

They will think the rug is grass and try to eat it.

They will also eat your mother's orchids.

They won't eat your little brother.

He'll still cry. Your mother will say,

You can tell them it's your little brother's fault. You will get sent to your room anyway. Your father will say,

MY FAVORITE PETS

BY GUS W.
FOR MS. SMOLINSKI'S CLASS

B+
Handwriting shows some improvement, Gus. Please tell yar mother thank you for the chocolates and new scarf.

Ms. Smolinski